Between Secrets and Shadows

Roy Herron

ISBN: 978-1-962204-85-9 (Paperback)

ISBN: 978-1-962204-86-6 (Hardcover)

Printed in United States of America

Contents

Chapter 1

A Spy's Dilemma

Sarah Morgan sat in her New Cross Central apartment in Manchester as she sipped on some Earl Grey tea. The walls of her room were adequately painted, and it seemed like the apartment had not been cleaned for days. Sarah stared at a file right in front of her. It said 'Classified' on the first page. Sarah knew what it was about. She had already been briefed about it by the Deputy Director of the MI6, James Mallory. She took another sip before leaning back onto the blue velvet chaise longue. She closed her eyes, and tried to relax before taking on the assignment.

Sarah Morgan had been a part of MI6 since the past fifteen years. She had joined the force in 2017, right after her mother's death. Since then, Sarah had operated from the dense jungles of the Amazon to the urbanized settings of Australia. She had seen death closely several times, but that never stopped her from serving her country. In fact, this is want she wanted to do. The excitement, the uncertainty, the high stakes were what kept Sarah going. Five years ago, she had rejected a desk job from the agency.

"I would rather retire than work behind a desk." Sarah had told her colleagues. "I'm field operative. It's in my blood. And it's not like I'm 60 years old."

The bureau had realized her significance and catered to her request. She was arguably the best agent that the MI6 had.

Sarah opened her eyes and took another sip of her tea. As she stared into the file, she got lost in thought. She remembered her time in Mozambique, where she was tailing an operative of ISIS-Mozambique. The guy was a local asset of the terror outfit, and Sarah had intelligence that he was facilitating in the preparation of a suicide attack in Maputo. Sarah watched him for days until one night, her apartment was ransacked. The insurgents were onto her. She was instructed to immediately fly back to the UK While on her way to the airport, she was attacked. Two Toyota pickups intercepted her Nissan Sunny as she somehow maneuvered her way to the airport. Sarah was shot in the arm.

She came back to the present again. Bringing her arm close to her body, she thought about how close of an encounter that was. *They were there to kidnap me. Not even the MI6 would have located me if they had gotten me.*

As an active duty agent, Sarah had been through so much worse, but this incident stuck with her. It still haunted her after seven years. She vividly remembered the face of the guy at the turret. He was dark, and had an untrimmed beard that made him look like a savage. His large, uneven teeth showed as he shouted at Sarah to pull over. When she refused to comply, the guy in the passenger seat took out a 9mm and shot her through the window.

She opened the file and examined it. It had a picture of Yuri Kazanovich. Yuri was a former FSB agent who had gone rogue, and was in possession of 'large amounts of Novichok.' The MI6 had intelligence that Kazanovich was in England, and was looking to sell the nerve agent to local gangs. The Albanians were most likely to be the largest buyers. Sarah skimmed through the file as she attempted to figure out the seriousness of the threat.

Sarah picked up her phone and dialed a number.

"Hey, there! How's the best agent in the MI6 feeling?" A voice said from the other end.

"Shut up, Rich. Did you get a chance to look at the Kazanovich file?"

"No, not really. What's up?"

"The usual. Ex-Russian intelligence guy trying to fuck with the West. Will the script ever change? And Novichok? Putin really needs to keep his men in control. This is gonna blow up right in his face. No one's gonna believe Kazanovich has gone rogue." Sarah seemed almost annoyed.

"You know how the Russians are. They're old school. Even we don't know for sure if Kazanovich's gone rogue."

"But the Kremlin's confirmed it."

"Sarah, did you join the force yesterday? Nine out of ten times, the Kremlin is bullshitting."

"So, you're saying Kazanovich is still taking orders from Moscow?"

"I'm just saying it could be that. Anyways, I'll take a look at the file, and I'll talk to you about it in detail."

"Alright." Sarah hung up.

Richard Lewinski and Sarah had gotten into the force together. Richard was the Director of Operations and one of the few bearable officers in the organization. Richard's career had progressed much faster than Sarah's. He had spent a substantial amount of time in the field, and had no retired to desk duty.

"I do this for Elena and the kids. You think I did not enjoy my time out there?" Richard said to Sarah a few days back.

"This is why I don't get attached to people. I can't compromise my job for one person. What's the point of loving someone if you have to let go of things that you have loved your entire life?" Sarah responded. Richard gave her a big smiling nod.

Sarah had grown up in London, and moved to Manchester when she was fifteen. Her parents were divorced and she grew up with her mother. At the time of her death, Sarah was stationed in

Venezuela. She could not attend her mother's funeral. Sarah regretted it, but she always felt it made her stronger. She did not let anything come in between her work, not even her own mother's death. In fact, her superiors said that she worked with even more focus after hearing the news of her mother passing away.

Sarah was always hungry for work. In fifteen years of service, she had never taken time off.

"Do terrorists take time off? Do our enemies go on holidays? They don't, so why should we?"

***

Alexander got out of the Boeing 777 at Heathrow International Airport. He took a deep sniff as soon as he exited the aircraft.

"The scent of English soil." He said to himself. Alex loved Europe. When he was stationed in Poland during the Russia-Ukraine War, he developed a liking for the continent. When Russia finally pulled its troops out of Ukraine after seven years, Alex put in a request to be transferred to somewhere in Europe only. He was sent to Austria to keep an eye on the reemergence of Al-Qaeda. He was PNG'd back to the United States after six months because of a tactical error that resulted in the death of 129 civilians in Graz.

Alexander got out of the airport and reached straight to the US embassy in London. As he entered the building, he felt a wave of excitement run through his body. He waited in the lobby for someone to receive him. After a few minutes, he was greeted by a tall man. He walked crisply toward Alex and was clad in a sky blue shirt.

"Alexander Davis?" He stretched out his hand.

"Hi, yes." Alex stood up.

"Jack Sullivan. Deputy COS. Come with me."

Alex followed him. The hallways echoed with the clicking of their heels.

"How was your flight?"

"It was, uh, okay. I guess. A bit turbulent."

"Well, yeah. The Atlantic is gonna somehow make you aware of its existence."

They both chuckled. Jack entered into a conference room as Alex followed him inside.

"Please, take a seat." Jack pointed to a chair as he sat down himself. "I would have loved us to get to know each other but we're a bit short on time. Before we meet the Matthew, let's go over a few things. Ever heard of Parker Prime?"

"Yeah, that's why I'm here."

"Well, you're gonna be here a while. We don't have anything on them yet. We're keeping an eye out. They're super discreet. They mainly run their operations through local assets. Popped up on our radar a few weeks back when they unloaded a large shipment of monitors from the docks. It came from South Sudan. That's all we know right now." Jack briefed Alex.

"Okay, well, doesn't seem like a threat serious enough to get the CIA involved."

"I haven't finished. You know Musab al Khubaib?"

"Al Quraishi's successor?"

"Exactly. We tracked the shipment back to one of his safe houses in Sudan. It gets complicated. The Sudanese RSF provides security to that safe house. We believe ISIS and Parker Prime are together in this."

"Wait. The RSF in South Sudan?

"Yes."

"Okay, and does Parker Prime have a history with terrorists?"

"We're trying to figure that out. The company seems legit on the surface. They claim to be financial analysts, which checks out. But this shipment has got us all on our feet."

"What about the MI6?" Alex asked.

"What about them? They're idiots. We can't trust them with this."

"Woah. I thought they were our allies."

"Sure, they tell the world that. But we don't leave things like these to them."

"But we're operating on British soil. We have to share intel with them, no?"

"Don't be naïve, kid. We only take them in when we have to take them in. Alright, 8am tomorrow. See you then." Jack left the room.

Alex sat in the room thinking about what Jack had just said. He immediately began working. His mind instinctively started creating scenarios. Alex took out his iPad and began making notes.

"Go home." Jack came back and peeked in from the door after a few seconds.

"Yeah, sorry." Alex got up and left the building.

Alex's alarm woke him up at 6:30 the next morning. His apartment was ten minutes away from the embassy. He quickly changed and had breakfast, two scrambled eggs, and a cup of decaf, something in his routine that had not changed in the past four years.

As Alex entered the embassy, he glanced at his wrist. *7:45.* He entered the building. It was nothing like the previous day. There must be at least seventy people in the lobby, which was practically empty when Jack came to him.

As he stopped outside the Chief of Station's room, he could not stop staring at the name plate. *Matthew Powell: Chief of Station, UK.* After a few seconds, he knocked and entered. Jack was already there and so was the COS.

"Alexander. Good Morning." Matthew said loudly.

"Good Morning, sir. Big fan."

"Yeah, a lot of people are." They all laughed. "Anyway, let's get to it. I believe Jack has gone over it with you?"

"Yes, sir."

"Alright, so, what do you think?"

"I did some digging on Parker Prime, made a few calls. They're execs have been involved with shady individuals in the past. Not directly but still. For example, this guy here." Alex took out a piece of paper from his briefcase. "Dylan Brooks. One of the Directors of Parker Prime. He funded the rebels in the Donbass region in 2021. He was also allegedly involved in the unrest in Sudan in 2023. He supported the RSF against the Sudanese Armed Forces. Here's a picture of him with Hemedti."

Matthew looked impressed. He looked at Alex and asked him what the next plan of action could be.

"We have to dig into Parker Prime. There has to be a loose end that connects them to Khubaib. Can we tap their phones?"

"We'll have to take MI5 into the loop if we do that." Jack interjected.

"Not necessarily. But yes that would be preferred."

"Because if we can do that, it might make our jobs a lot easier." Alex said.

"Alright, let's see what we can do regarding that. Anything else?"

"Not yet, but I'm hoping to find something concrete in the next few days. We had almost an identical scenario when I was in Poland. So this isn't new for me. I know how they operate." Alex said confidently.

Chapter 2

The Intricate Web

Sarah got out of the house and sat in the cab. She looked at her watch. *7:37.* Her flight was at 9:15 but she always felt comfortable reaching the airport a bit early. Sarah took out her phone and found a message from Richard.

When are you reaching?

Sarah threw her phone in her bag without responding. She peeked outside as the car raced past the streets of Manchester. Once at the airport, she quickly checked-in, waited for her boarding. Within a few minutes, she could see a Ryanair Boeing 737 taxiing on the tarmac. Sarah picked up her bag and boarded the flight.

Two hours and something minutes later, the flight landed. As soon as Sarah got out of the aircraft, her phone rang. It was Richard.

"Hey, how do you like it?"

"Like what?"

"Prague."

"Shut up, Rich. Where are you?"

"Right outside. In the lot. White Honda Fit. There aren't many cars here. You'll see me."

Sarah disconnected the call and moved toward the exit. She quickly spotted a White Honda Fit, and sat in it. She stared at Richard for a few seconds.

"Why the fuck are we in Prague?" She asked.

"Whoa, easy! And yeah, I have no idea. Mallory is waiting for us. Maybe he can let us in on some useful information." Richard laughed.

"I hate these higher-ups sometimes, I swear." Sarah said, visibly annoyed.

The two drove for about twenty five minutes before coming to a stop outside a small bungalow. The street seemed much quieter than the rest of the city. The house itself was old, and not too welcoming. Sarah looked at Richard.

"This is the location I got." Richard shrugged his shoulders.

"I swear to God, if this is a safe house, I'm gonna quit this mission, whatever it is."

"Nah, you won't." Richard laughed as they both entered the house. Sarah looked around, walking slowly toward the briefing room. The house looked old from inside. Sarah could see seepage on the walls. It seemed as if it hadn't been painted it years, and the design of the interior showed that it was a Cold War era building.

They both entered a room to find Vincent Mallory sitting on the table. It seemed as if he was waiting for them only. He was clad in a pain black polo and jeans. His shaved head and big glasses made him seem cartoonish. Mallory was the head of operations of the MI6 in the Czech Republic.

"Sir." Richard stretched out his hand.

"You're late." Mallory said without reciprocating the handshake. "Anyways, let's get to it. We just received intel that the some insurgent groups from the Middle East have arrived here in Prague. They're having a little tea party tomorrow somewhere in the city. Find out what they're up to." Mallory stood up to leave.

"Wait, that's it?" Sarah asked.

"Actually, no. There's one more thing. This place, it's a safe house. Make yourself comfortable." Mallory left the room.

"Wow. Just…wow." Sarah looked at Richard.

"I thought you loved your time out in the field." Richard said mockingly.

"I do. But why can't they give us better safe houses." Sarah complained.

"Better safe houses? What do you want? A mansion?"

"Fuck off, Rich. Why are you here anyway? Why aren't you sitting on your ass in London behind a desk?"

"I was here to debrief a team on another assignment. Mallory called me out of the blue and asked me to pick you up from the airport."

Sarah seemed annoyed. She picked up a random crystal dolphin that was not contributing to the dull ambience at all. She began to fidget.

"And what about the Yuri case?"

"We've been told that that case isn't too 'urgent'." Richard said.

Sarah picked up a file kept on the table. She opened it and saw the details of the operation. Sarah immediately closed it and threw herself on the bed. She decided to catch some sleep before working on the project.

Sarah woke up a couple of hours later, and got to work. She made herself a cup of black coffee and sat down to research on the group. She opened the file again.

Al-Shanashi is a brutal terrorist group with origins in Syria. It is essentially Bashar al Assad's private military contractor. Al-

Shanashi had been involved in numerous attacks on civilians within, and outside the borders of Syria.

Sarah quickly turned a few pages.

Objective: Infiltrate Al-Shanashi's meeting in Prague. Do not engage. This is an intelligence gathering mission.

The file had almost everything that the MI6 had on Al-Shanashi. Sarah went back to the first page and began reading it thoroughly. After several hours of intense research, which included making some calls, she went to bed.

The crisp morning air sent a shiver down Sarah's spine as she stepped out of the safe house into the bustling streets of Prague. The city's ancient charm was juxtaposed with the urgency of her mission. She adjusted the collar of her coat. The familiar weight of her concealed weapons providing a semblance of comfort. A Glock was all that she needed to protect herself, but the agency had certain requirements.

The intelligence she had gathered the previous night pointed to a clandestine meeting at an abandoned warehouse in Krakovská. The area was known one of the shadiest places in the city. It was a crucial link in the chain that connected the terrorist plot to its financiers. Sarah knew that unraveling this part of the puzzle would bring her one step closer to the truth.

With each passing minute, her determination grew stronger. She couldn't afford to let any distractions cloud her judgment. The stakes were too high, and the lives of countless innocent people hung in the balance.

At the warehouse, Sarah surveyed the area from a safe vantage point. She could see a small group of heavily armed individuals entering the building, their hushed voices and cautious movements indicating the gravity of their mission. She knew she had to infiltrate the meeting undetected, gathering vital information without raising suspicion.

Drawing on her extensive training, Sarah formulated a plan. She would use her expertise in disguise and subterfuge to blend in seamlessly. With a new identity and a cover story ready, she made her way towards the warehouse, her heart pounding with adrenaline.

Sarah managed to sneak to the back of the warehouse, climbing on the roof. Undetected, she slid down from one of the skylights that led her to an empty part of the warehouse. It was dimly lit, but Sarah could manage to make her way around it.

She could hear muffled voices from somewhere close. She moved closer to the voices and found a spot from where she could hear them clearly. She peeked inside, and figured that she could actually enter the room and stand at such a place that no one would really notice her. She would be hiding in plain sight. Sarah analyzed the entire situation for two seconds, and then proceeded with her plan.

The room was filled with tension, a palpable undercurrent of danger. She discreetly observed the attendees, analyzing their body language and searching for familiar faces.

Then, she spotted a figure in the corner, his presence sending a jolt through her. She did not know him, and in her mind, he was most definitely one of the bad guys. But there was something about him that Sarah found quite enticing. She stared at him for a few seconds before turning her attention back to the people in the room.

He stood with an air of confidence, effortlessly commanding attention. Sarah's heart skipped a beat as their eyes briefly met. The intensity of that fleeting connection sent her mind into overdrive. Was he here as an ally or an adversary? She couldn't be certain, but her instincts told her that his presence held significance.

Sarah had never felt anything like this before, especially not on a mission. She was focusing on the meeting but this mere feeling was enough to get her distracted.

As the meeting commenced, Sarah listened intently, her ears tuned to every word spoken. Fragments of information floated around the room—code names, locations, and cryptic references that hinted at a larger, more sinister plan. She jotted down notes, committing each detail to memory, determined to piece together the puzzle that had consumed her existence.

Suddenly, a commotion erupted at the far end of the room. Chaos ensued as armed men stormed the warehouse, weapons drawn. The loud echoes of XM11s could heard all over as shouts in English and Arabic overlapped. The attackers were dressed in all black, with their faces covered by protective gear. They seemed like professionals.

Sarah instinctively sought cover, her training kicking in as she assessed the situation. The tranquility of the meeting had been shattered, replaced by a frantic scramble for survival. The members of the meetings picked up their own weapons and fired indiscriminately in the room.

Amidst the chaos, Sarah caught a glimpse of the same man, his eyes locking with hers for an instant. There was a flicker of understanding, a shared recognition that they were both caught in a dangerous game. With a nod, they silently agreed to a temporary truce, their individual goals temporarily aligned. Sarah and the man fought their way through the mayhem, their skills as agents honed to perfection.

Together, they navigated the maze of gunfire and chaos, their movements synchronized in a deadly dance. In this battlefield of shadows, their alliance became an unspoken testament to the complexities of their connection.

After several minutes of intense fighting, Sarah signaled him to follow her. She led him to the room from where she had slid in. The skylight was still open and Sarah jumped onto the ladder and began climbing. The man followed her. They reached the top of the roof and managed to get down to the ground escaping into the distance as the warehouse burned behind them.

The two could still here gunfire behind them as they ran. They ran for about a kilometer before coming to a stop, temporarily finding refuge in a secluded alley. Their adrenaline-fueled breathing was the only sound in the stillness. Facing each other, the two acknowledged the fragile trust they had formed, knowing that their paths might continue to intersect.

"Sarah." Sarah stretched her hand.

"Alexander."

Sarah was impressed by his grip. Something told her that Alexander was on the same mission as her. Without putting much thought into it, Sarah decided to find out who he was.

"What were you doing there?" Sarah blurted out. Alexander was still a little out of breath.

"Do you really expect me to answer that?" Alex asked.

"What are you? CIA? FSB? Mossad?" Sarah interrogated further. Alexander just smiled.

"Good fight out there." He walked away. Sarah stared at him until he disappeared from sight.

Chapter 3

The Hunt Begins

Sarah sat alone in the dimly lit safe house, her mind consumed by the enigmatic encounter with Alexander Davis. His piercing blue eyes lingered in her thoughts, his words echoing through her mind like a haunting melody. The stale smell that engulfed the entire safe house made Sarah sick. She felt like she could not think straight. Maybe that is why she was fan-girling over Alexander.

Sarah had always prided herself on her ability to detach emotionally from her targets, but something about him stirred a deep and unfamiliar longing within her. And although she had interacted with him for barely ten minutes, she just could not get him out of her mind.

As she sipped her lukewarm coffee, a wave of conflicting emotions washed over Sarah. How could she reconcile her growing feelings for a man who could be her potential enemy? For all she knew, Alexander could be in cahoots with the terrorists. The lines between friend and foe had blurred, leaving her in a tangled web of uncertainty. Trusting her instincts had always served her well in the field, but this situation was unlike anything she had ever encountered.

The mission at hand demanded her attention. The agency had uncovered a high-profile terrorist plot, and Sarah was assigned to dismantle the terrorist network responsible. She needed to focus, but her mind kept drifting back to Alexander. His allure was undeniable, and the dangerous dance they were engaged in only heightened the intensity of their connection.

Hours turned into days as Sarah immersed herself in gathering intelligence, her determination fueling her every move. She traveled from one city to another, discreetly infiltrating secret hideouts and covert meetings. Each step brought her closer to unraveling the intricate web of deceit that threatened global security.

But the more Sarah delved into the heart of the conspiracy, the more she realized that the lines between good and evil were not as clear-cut as she had been led to believe. A startling realization began to dawn on her—the true enemy might not be who she thought it was. With every piece of information she uncovered, a larger puzzle emerged, and the stakes grew higher.

Amidst the chaos and danger, Sarah's thoughts kept circling back to Alexander. She wondered if he too was questioning his loyalties. Were they both mere pawns in a much larger game? Their paths had intertwined for a reason, and Sarah couldn't shake the feeling that there was more to their connection than meets the eye. She wondered whether she would run into Alexander ever again. Something from within told her that he was around, and that they would meet again soon.

***

Sarah entered a dark street in west Pilsen. Her Citroen C1 silently cruised through a street as Sarah looked carefully at the buildings on the left side of the street. The buildings seemed eerily empty although Sarah knew that people lived there. She looked for the apartment where she knew a meet was happening. As Sarah moved toward the end of the street, she saw a faint light emanating from the building. She parked her car down the road and looked around, not a man in sight.

Sarah took out her Glock from the glove box, and put on the suppressor. Without making any noise, she got out of the car and moved toward the dimly lit apartment. Sarah reached at the entrance.

Fucking-A!

The door was locked. She looked around, hoping to find an alternative route. There was none.

What the fuck would I done entering the building anyway? I'm not here to conduct a fucking raid.

Sarah spotted a pipe running up the building. She put the Glock in the holster and assessed the pipe. Once she was sure that the pipe could hold her weight, Sarah began to climb carefully knowing that even a slight noise could alert them. It took her a minute to climb up to the second floor. She managed to jump onto a ledge and walk to the window.

Sarah had to be careful. Whoever was in there, if they saw her peeking inside, her life could be in danger. Slowly, she took out a small mirror, and placed it in front of the window. There were three men inside, none facing directly toward the window. Sarah pushed the mirror closer. She repositioned her earpiece. The men were speaking Arabic. For the millionth time, Sarah expressed gratitude for knowing Arabic.

"We'll keep them stored at the post only when the shipment comes in tomorrow evening. Makes no sense to unload it and bring it in the city, and then load it again."

"What if the Prague Smíchov port authorities find it?"

"They're not going to pry much. I'll make sure."

Suddenly, the men went silent. Before Sarah could figure out why, she heard one of the men speak.

"What the fuck?"

She looked in the mirror. He had spotted the mirror and the microphone, and was walking towards it. Sarah knew she had to run. It took her less than twenty seconds to reach to the pipe and slide her way down. As she ran back to her car, she heard the man shout from the window. Sarah knew he could be armed. As she sat in her car, a bullet flew through her rear windscreen. She started the car screeched her way out of the street, constantly glancing at her rearview mirror. She could see the silhouette of the man in the window.

Sarah reached the safe house a few minutes later. She had been extra cautious coming back. Not only did she have to make sure that she wasn't being followed, but she also had to avoid the police. If a police car had spotted a bullet hole in her windscreen, she could have been in trouble. Sarah parked the car inside the garage and went inside.

She threw herself on the couch and let out a loud sigh. Almost immediately, she dialed up Richard. It went straight to voicemail. Sarah kept on calling until Richard answered about half an hour later.

"Jeez. Relax. Eighteen calls? Has Kim launched nukes at America?" Richard laughed.

"Shut up. Listen to me. Al-Shanashi's getting a shipment tomorrow."

"Okay, and?" Richard's voice turned serious.

"Prague Smíchov Port. Tomorrow evening. They plan to hold the shipment at the port only before they move it forward."

"Forward?"

"Yeah, they were talking about how it won't make sense to bring it inside the city if they have to re-ship it," Sarah spoke quickly.

"Do you know what the shipment is?" Richard quickly grabbed a notebook and the pencil.

"No, they spotted me before I could get more information."

"Spotted you?" Richard asked loudly. "They've seen your face?"

"No, of course not. They just know someone was there listening to them. I escaped immediately." Sarah deliberately left out the part where her car was shot upon.

"Okay, I'll move this forward," Richard said.

"Do you want me to go to the docks tomorrow?" Sarah asked plainly. Richard went quiet for a moment.

"No, let the agents on the ground handle it."

"Am I not an agent on the ground?"

"I mean, we'll send in a combat team. They'll handle it," Richard responded. "And Sarah, be careful."

"Yeah." Sarah cut the call.

Combat team, my ass. I did this. I'm not gonna let some pricks with guns take all the credit.

She picked up her bag, and left for the train station. As Sarah boarded the train, all she could think about was Alexander.

I escaped death a few minutes ago. I'm on my way to ambush a shipment from the largest terrorist organization in the world. I haven't slept properly in days. And what is at the front of my mind? Fucking Alexander.

She smiled and shook her head as she looked down. Sarah stood on the precipice of a life-altering decision. She could follow the path she had always known, staying loyal to her agency and fulfilling her duty. Or she could take a leap of faith, trusting her instincts and the unexpected bond she shared with a man who she had met just once.

In this world of shadows and deception, where every step brought new revelations and dangers, Sarah had to find the strength to make the right choice. With her heart and country hanging in the balance, she knew the path ahead would be treacherous. The intricate web of lies and secrets would bind her tighter or ensnare her completely.

As Sarah prepared herself for the showdown, she couldn't help but wonder: would love be her salvation or her downfall? The answer remained uncertain, but one thing was certain—her fate and Alexander's were now inextricably intertwined, and their choices would shape the world around them.

***

"Alex, are you ready?" A voice asked from the other side of the phone.

"Yes, sir," Alexander replied, trying to put on his left shoe. He was late. Although, the rendezvous point was five minutes away from Alex's safe house, he knew he should have been there earlier. He quickly put on his shoes, and left.

The meeting point was another safe house. As Alex entered into the house, he saw four men standing around a table. One of them turned around and greeted Alex. He was bald, and had an earpiece on him. Alex immediately recognized him.

"David Blair?"

"Alexander Davis!"

"What the hell are you doing in Europe?" Alex asked as they casually hugged. "And I called you 'sir', on the phone? Un-fucking-believable." David and Alex laughed.

"Let me brief us on the operation. You three, this is Alex. Alex, Michael, Shane, and Joe." David pointed to the three men respectively. "We'll catch up later. I'm here in Prague for at least a month," David said, looking at Alex. "So, we've got intel that a shipment for Al-Shanashi is coming in. We don't have any details except that the shipment won't be off loaded. Their plan is to hold it at the port, and then ship it to another place some days later. Your objective, is to identify the shipment. Any questions?" David looked around.

"A lot," Alex said.

"Well, too bad, that's all we have. What we don't have is time. Good luck."

Alex and the three men got into a black Skoda Octavia and left. As they reached the port, they spotted a black van parked at a distance. Alex looked at Shane in the passenger seat. There was consensus that the van was shady.

The four men exited the car and walked inside the terminal. The port was relatively quieter. It had an odd vibe to it. They spotted a crane unloading some containers from a ship. Alex signaled to the other men, and they all went toward the ship.

As they sneakily approached the spot, they hid themselves behind a container from where they could see what was happening. Suddenly, the heard footsteps behind them. Before even turning around, all four of them brandished their pistols.

Alex spotted a shadow behind him but before he could do anything, someone fired at them. Alex ducked and took cover behind another container while his teammates attempted to thwart the gunfire of an MP5 with their pistols.

Suddenly, Alex heard a yell followed by a thud. He looked toward them and saw Michael lying on the floor. He had been shot in the head. Alex just stared at him. It was after years that he had saw a man die in front of him. In those years, Alex had always thought he had become immune to seeing death, but that wasn't it. Seeing a bullet lodged into Michael's head paralyzed Alex. He had not fully gained his composure when Shane and Joe also went down. Alex immediately radioed David.

"Alpha 3 to base, Alpha 3 to base, do you copy?" Alex said in a low voice.

"Alpha 3, we read you. Go ahead."

"They're dead. They're all fucking dead."

Before anyone could reply, a bullet hit the container right above Alex. He ran in the opposite direction to hide. He could hear the men shout in a language that he did not recognize.

"Quick, come with me." Alex heard a voice behind him. It was definitely a familiar voice, but who could it be at this time and place? He turned around to find Sarah. Without putting any thought into it, he followed her. They navigated through the maze of containers for a few minutes before getting out of the port.

Once they were at a safe distance, they stopped at a secluded building. Alex was out of breath. He bent down and put his hands on his knees. He had so many questions. After a few minutes of sitting in silence, Alex looked up at the girl who had just saved her life.

Chapter 4

Unmasking Deceptions

"Base to Alpha 3, do you copy?" There was static in Alexander's radio. He was still looking at Sarah as he took out his radio.

"This is Alpha 3. Go ahead."

"What the fuck happened, Alex?" David said from the other end.

"They're dead. The other three."

"What do you mean they're dead? Did I not categorically instruct you all to 'identify' the shipment?"

"What are you giving me shit for? They fired at us out of nowhere." Alex sounded angry.

"Where are-" Before David could complete, Alex's radio died. He looked up at Sarah again. They stared at each other for a few seconds, their eyes locked, silently acknowledging the dangerous dance they were engaged in. The encounter at the port had brought them closer, but their allegiances remained uncertain.

"What were you doing at the port?" Sarah broke the silence, her voice laced with a mixture of caution and curiosity.

"I know you just saved my life, and you think I owe it to you, but that is a question that I cannot answer right now," Alex replied.

"Listen to me, Alexander. Did I get that right?"

Alex nodded.

"I think we're on the same side here. But we won't know for sure unless we communicate. So, let me ask you again, what were you doing at the port?" Sarah asked.

"Why don't we start with you, huh? What were you doing there?"

Sarah paused for a few seconds before speaking.

"Al-Shanashi," Sarah replied. "I was there to identify a shipment, a container." She took out a card from her back pocket and almost shoved it in Alex's face. "MI6. I wasn't supposed to be there though. My CO told me not to go."

Alexander looked at her and gave a slight nod. She kept the card back in her pocket.

"You're still not gonna tell me?" Sarah asked. Alexander shrugged his shoulders. "Are we on the same side?" Alexander's gaze softened, his features betraying a hint of vulnerability.

"Our paths have crossed for a reason, Sarah. Trust is a precious commodity in our line of work, but something about you has stirred emotions I thought I had long buried," Alexander said.

Sarah's heart skipped a beat, her instincts warring with her training. She had been taught to trust no one, yet an undeniable connection between them transcended the boundaries of their respective roles. She felt something very strongly but chose not to display her emotions yet.

"I ask you who you're working for, and you're getting all emotional?"

"Ummm, yeah. Sorry. That was weird." Alex chuckled nervously.

"Tell me, Alexander," she implored, her voice barely above a whisper, "what are you truly after? Is there more to this mission than meets the eye?"

A pensive expression crossed Alexander's face as he weighed his words carefully. "There's a web of deception at play, Sarah. The true enemy is not who we have been led to believe. Higher powers are manipulating the strings, and they'll stop at nothing to achieve their nefarious goals. We're merely pawns in their game."

"What do you mean?" Sarah asked, curiosity engulfing her face.

"Can I trust you, Sarah?" Alexa asked almost immediately.

"You have no reason to. But yes, you can," Sarah responded plainly.

"I'm with the CIA. Been with them since years now."

"Yeah, I figured."

"Really? How?" Alex asked.

"I knew you were American. That narrowed it down pretty much. Anyways," Sarah casually responded. She could feel something for him especially when he showed that he trusted her.

"I've kept this from the agency, but this Al-Shanashi, it's not your regular terrorist group."

"You also like to defy orders? Nice." Sarah chuckled lightly. "Anyways, what do you mean when you say regular terrorist group?"

"Sit." Alexander pointed to a cement block. They both sat down as Alex took a few seconds to resume. "Ever heard of Parker Prime?" Sarah shook her head. "They're financial analysts registered in the Cayman Islands, headquartered in London. A few weeks back, they unloaded a shipment in the UK. Monitors. They came from a safe house in South Sudan."

"And?" Sarah's curiosity had now peaked.

"The safe house is owned by ISIS leader Musab al Khubaib." Alex could see the excitement in Sarah's eyes.

"And what about Al-Shanashi? Where do they fit into all of this?"

"Just another name for ISIS."

"Wait, so you're saying that Parker Prime and ISIS are hand in hand. And the CIA doesn't know that?"

"They think they're together but I know for sure. I did some digging on my own. I know for a fact that ISIS and Parker Prime are working together. Or at least were."

"Why do you say that?"

"Because those soldiers we saw at the warehouse the other day? They were Parker Prime's men. That means Prime and Shanashi, or ISIS, had some sort of a fall out. I'm trying to figure out that part."

"And why aren't you going to the Agency with this information?"

"Fucking bureaucracy. Slows everything down. I'm gonna get it done on my own." Alex seemed annoyed.

Sarah's mind raced, assimilating this new information. The world she thought she understood had crumbled around her, leaving her stranded in a fog of uncertainty. The mission that had initially seemed so straightforward now revealed layers of complexity she had never anticipated.

With a determined glint in her eyes, Sarah made up her mind. "If we want to uncover the truth, we must delve deeper, and expose the puppeteers who control our destinies. Together, we have a better chance of exposing their plans."

Alexander nodded, a rare smile playing at the corners of his lips. "Agreed, Sarah. We can't allow our personal feelings to cloud our judgment, but we can use our shared connection to our advantage. Let's pool our resources and expose the true puppet masters orchestrating this intricate game of shadows."

Before Sarah could respond, they heard a vehicle approach the building. They immediately hid behind a wall and waited in silence. A few seconds later, the vehicle halted near the building. They heard a door open and then slam shut. Alexander could hear his heart pounding as he saw the nervousness on Sarah's face as well. These were the agents who would not flinch even if they had a gun to their face. But perhaps, the emotional connection that they had established was doing unprecedented things to them.

"Alex, are you here?" David shouted. Alex took a sigh of relief. He told Sarah to run away undetected.

"Wait. How do I contact you?" Sarah whispered. Alex quickly took Sarah's phone and dialed in her number. A couple of seconds later, he came out of his hiding place. David instinctively pointed his gun toward him.

"Hey, hey. Easy."

"What the fuck happened, Alex?" David asked, putting his Glock back in its holster.

Alex narrated the entire story, leaving out the part where Sarah rescued him. He knew it would get complicated. And he still didn't trust Sarah enough.

"Are you okay?" David put his hand on Alex's shoulder.

"Yeah, I guess."

Sarah could hear the entire conversation from the other side of the wall. As soon as she heard them leave, she came out of the shadows and disappeared into the distance.

It was around seven in the evening. Sarah sat in her safe house, thinking about her previous day's interaction with Alex. She just could not get her mind off of Alex. She kept reminiscing the moment when he asked if he could trust her.

Is this what love feels like? Or am I just being overly dramatic. Don't be an idiot, Sarah! You've got so much more important shit to take care of. You're not a fuckin' schoolgirl. Why are you fantasizing about a random boy? Exactly! I'm not a schoolgirl, and even then I'm feeling whatever this is. Should I call him?

Sarah knew there was no other way to contact him. She contemplated whether she should call him or not. After a few minutes, she picked up her phone and dialed his number.

Alex was sitting in his balcony having a smoke. He, too, had been thinking about Sarah since last night. He thought about how he had expressed his feelings to her openly, and how well she had handled the situation. As he exhaled another puff into the dark sky, his phone rang.

Just let me be at peace for a while, for Christ's sake.

"Alex," he said, seemingly annoyed.

"Hey," A voice answered form the other side.

"Sarah?"

"Yeah. I hope I'm not disturbing you."

"No, not at all. How are you?"

"I'm good. Just a little restless. Can't get over what you-"

"Yeah, yeah. Absolutely." Alex cut her off. "Listen, do you wanna meet right now?"

"Yeah, sure. I'll send you my address." Sarah paused for a second. "Actually, let's meet at the Donuterie. Does that work?" Sarah did not trust him enough just yet to let him know the location of his safe house.

"The café? Yeah, sure. I'll be there in twenty." Alex got dressed and headed out.

About half an hour later, they met at the busy café in almost the middle of the city. They talked about their time in their respective agencies, and explained how they got to this point. After a while, Sarah brought up Parker Prime again.

"That's all I know. What I told you yesterday," Alex responded.

"But how can a company headquartered in London be involved with ISIS? What on Earth is MI5 doing?"

"It's on their radar. But they haven't done anything substantial to stop it yet."

The two discussed the case for about an hour. Sarah found herself lost in the discussion many times. She could not compute the words coming out of Alex's mouth. There was magic in his eyes that Sarah could just not ignore. Alex, too, was on the same wavelength. And although, he concealed it quite nicely, it did not suppress what he was feeling from within.

"You wanna work on this together?" Alex asked Sarah. "Two heads are better than one."

"Absolutely." Sarah immediately agreed. She was still angry about the fact that Richard had disallowed her to be at the docks.

The duo forged an alliance right in the middle of the cafe. People around them were oblivious to the fact that their fate lay in the hands of these two ordinary looking agents. Alex and Sarah's paths had converged in a union of shared purpose.

As they agreed on dealing with this threat together, they realized the dangers they would face and the sacrifices they might have to make. Once a fragile thread, trust began to weave itself into the fabric of their partnership.

They knew that their journey would take them to the heart of the intelligence community, where they would need to manipulate the shadows, piecing together fragments of information, and leveraging their skills to dismantle the network of lies. Neither of them was unfamiliar to that.

In fact, they both felt a wave of excitement go through them. Taking down a potential global level terror outfit combined with a flurry of emotions was something they had never encountered before. Like always, they had to be prepared to encounter unexpected allies and formidable adversaries, each encounter further illuminating the vast conspiracy they were up against.

Sarah and Alexander found themselves on the edge of a precipice. The choices they would make in the coming days would determine not only their fates but also the destiny of nations.

In the heart-pounding race against time, they were prepared to risk everything—their lives, loyalties, and the burgeoning romance that had unexpectedly blossomed between them. Love could become their greatest strength or their most vulnerable weakness in this realm of spies, enemies, and entangled hearts.

Chapter 5

The Unholy Duo

The atmosphere at the headquarters in Langley was tensed. CIA Deputy Director John Mattis sat in his office across David Blair and Cameron Roberts. He was visibly concerned about what had happened in Prague, his fingers oscillating back and forth against each other. After a few seconds, he looked up at them.

"What the hell happened?" John asked in a loud voice.

"Sir, they were ambushed," Cameron responded. She was the longest serving Deputy Chief of Station in Czechoslovakia yet.

"By who? Did we not have intel? Three CIA operatives are dead. The guy on the seventh floor is gonna be on my ass. He's gonna want answers," John responded plainly.

"We believe it was someone other than ISIS. We're finding out who it was, sir." David adjusted himself in the compact chair.

"Have something for me by tomorrow."

David and Cameron left the office, lightly closing the door behind them. As they walked through the broad corridor, David looked at Cameron.

"Any idea who it could be?"

"Could be a splinter group, a rogue faction within *Da'esh.* Let's see." Cameron turned right as David stopped there only. He knew Cameron was pissed at him. He watched her walk away into the distance. David let out a huge sigh and left the building.

***

"How do you do know if you can trust me?" Sarah asked as she entered into Alexander's apartment.

"What do you mean? Please." He pointed toward the sofa.

"This is your safe house, I'm assuming?"

"It isn't actually. I've rented this place. I come here when the work gets too much. Whiskey?" Alex help up a bottle of Blanton's.

"Sure. You can find this stuff here?" Sarah laughed.

"Of course. This isn't the Czech Republic anymore." Alex poured her a glass.

"You're not having any?" Sarah asked sipping on her glass.

"Nah, too early for me."

"2 pm is too early for you?"

"Yeah. I can't think straight if I even have a sip. So I save it for later at night. Anyways."

"So, what do we have on Parker Prime and ISIS?"

"A CI in Syria told me there's been a major disruption in the organizational structure of ISIS. He said something about a coup from within. They tried to remove al-Khubaib, and he cracked down on the conspirators. Some of them fled and joined other smaller groups like the AQI." Alex paused to look at Sarah. He pretended that he was giving her a moment to comprehend what he said but it was her eyes that made him stop. He was simply in awe.

"Okay, and?"

Sarah's voice brought him back to his senses.

"Yeah so, he also told me that those who had fled had information about Parker Prime and ISIS working together. So now, we have other smaller extremist factions going after whatever it was in that shipment. People who fired at us, they were probably part of those groups. They managed to reach there before Parker Prime's men," Alex explained.

"What now?" Sarah's eyes widened. Alex slid a file to Sarah. She put down the glass and opened it. Sarah's face showed no expression. "What's Maelstrom?" She looked at Alex.

"It's a long story. But this entire thing just got a hell lot complicated," Alex replied. "Back in the 60s, when Khrushchev was in power, the Soviets initiated a program called 'Maelstrom.' It was overseen directly by the Kremlin. They wanted to take over the West in a rather unorthodox manner."

"Which was what?" Sarah sat upright.

"The Soviets wanted to get into the heads of leaders of the West."

"And? I mean, we all know how effective KGB propaganda was."

"Not that. They literally wanted to get into their heads. As in, control their minds. The idea was to 'push a button in Moscow and force decisions to be taken in the West, particularly the US."

Sarah let out a laugh.

"That is the most absurd thing I have ever heard."

"It is. But it kinda worked. The Russians made some kind of a device that could practically hypnotize you. Anyways, the program was dropped when Khrushchev got out of office. My theory? This shit with Parker Prime and ISIS, it's Maelstrom resurfacing. Only this time, Maelstrom isn't just an initiative. It's a whole fucking organization." Alex poured himself a drink.

"Wow. It must be something to get you to drink in the day," Sarah chuckled.

"When I was stationed in Russia, we heard chatter about how a group of Russian oligarchs, tight with Putin, were working on something similar. We looked into it, but it seemed like a dead end. I'm convinced it is that only."

"If I'm being honest, I think it's a little far-fetched. But continue." She took another sip.

"I intercepted this one call from a big oil guy. Some executive of Gazprom, Yuri Kazanovich. He said, quote 'Are the monitors ready for a test run?' To which the other guy replied that they were. That was it. Maybe I'm reading too much into it but I have a feeling that it is this only."

"Yuri Kazanovich?" Sarah yelled.

"Yeah, why?"

"Jesus! I was working on him before this case. We have intel that he's carrying around Novichok around England, looking for the highest bidder. I need to report this back to London." Sarah picked up her phone.

"No, no, no. Wait. I think we can get to it before our departments can. We can help each other out. What do you say?" Alex asked.

"This is gonna be treason. We have to report it to our superiors."

"We will, of course, at the right time."

For some reason, Sarah was convinced. Something inside of her told her that she should listen to Alex. Maybe it was his charm. Maybe she was too mesmerized by his presence.

"Okay, fine. What now?"

"I have some contacts in Russia. Let me see if I can find something." He picked up his phone and stepped out of the room. Sarah could hear him speak from inside. Alex stepped in after a few minutes. "Bingo!"

"You speak Russian?"

"Since I was a kid," Alex almost bragged. "You're more interested in my Russian than what I have to tell you?"

"Maybe." Sarah smiled. "What is it?"

"The guy just told me that the Russian government bought a place in Austria. He doesn't know what it's for but he seemed pretty sure it was for something shady. He's also heard recently that Maelstrom is resurfacing. He doesn't have a clue what it is. Just said he thought I should know." Alex was visibly excited.

Sarah did not respond. She just stared at Alex, feeling a strong connection. Alex also locked eyes with her, seemingly paralyzed. Suddenly, something shook Sarah. She shrugged off her thoughts and looked at the file again.

"MI6 is a shitty place but I really think you should take this to the CIA."

"Okay well, I'll just tell you. I did take it to the CIA. They laughed it off. Literally laughed it off. I've stopped taking them seriously after that. During those two months, I was practically living at Langley and the White House. And in the end, they just wrote it off. I'm not gonna have them waste my time again."

Sarah nodded.

They boarded the next train to Graz, unaware of what they would find. Over the course of the next two months, Alex and Sarah's feelings for each other grew rapidly. As they spent more and more time working together, a powerful force seemed to fire their emotions.

Chapter 6

Unexpected Alliances

Sarah and Alexander sat in the same apartment in Prague where they started their chase of Maelstrom. After travelling almost the entire Europe, parts of South America, and the Middle East, they had collected substantial intel on Maelstrom. They knew that they stood on the edge of a breakthrough, their shared determination propelling them forward. They had uncovered a tangled web of corruption, betrayal, and hidden agendas that reached the highest levels of power.

Maelstrom had their men everywhere. From the US Congress to the guerilla forces deep in the Amazon. They had penetrated every power corridor, regardless of its magnitude. With every revelation, their understanding of the true enemy deepened.

"It's an elusive organization that operates in the shadows, manipulating world events for its gain." Sarah looked at Alex. "How is this to define Maelstrom?"

"What are you doing?" Alex asked.

"Preparing a report to present to the agency," she responded.

"Not yet, Sarah. Trust me. We need to have a closer look at Maelstrom before we involve our agencies."

"You sure?" Sarah asked.

Alex nodded.

"What's next? We have everything we need."

"We need a cunning strategy, and an unexpected level of cooperation."

"Cooperation? From who?"

"Each other. We need to be together like we have been in the last two months. We need to seek allies within the intelligence community. MI6, CIA, Mossad, no resource is a bad resource right now. Except for the Russians of course. And we need to make sure we only use personal connections who would not leak any information to their superiors. If the Mossad gets its hands on our case file, it wouldn't take them a second to share it with Washington," Alex said with determination.

"So you're saying we need to 'recruit' people, if that's the right word, like us? Agents who are tired of all the procedures and stuff?"

"Exactly! People who can defy their superiors to do the right thing. We don't want a bunch of idiots taking orders from elected buffoons."

"But we need to be careful. We can't just take anyone on board. We need to steer clear of the FSB and Maelstrom. And the way Maelstrom is operating, I'm beginning to think even you work for them," Sarah laughed.

"No, you're right. We need to be extra careful."

Sarah and Alexander knew that trust was a fragile currency, and they had to tread carefully. Each person they approached was a potential double agent or a pawn in Maelstrom's game. Sarah's instincts, honed through years of training, guided her choices. She sought individuals with a fire in their eyes, a deep-rooted belief in justice, and a yearning for redemption.

Over the next few weeks, Sarah and Alexander began to assemble their team. They hired hackers, soldiers belonging to ex-special forces of different countries, and even retired politicians who still had enough influence to sway the decisions of present governments. The diverse group faced skepticism and suspicion. But Sarah's unwavering determination and Alexander's enigmatic charisma slowly won over the hearts and minds of those who had grown disillusioned with the system.

Together, they formed an unlikely alliance, each member bringing unique skills and perspectives to the table. With their combined knowledge and resources, they began to chip away at Maelstrom's façade, exposing its operatives and unmasking its darkest secrets.

The battles they fought were not only physical but also psychological. Maelstrom struck back with cunning, launching counterattacks and spreading disinformation to sow seeds of doubt within their ranks. Sarah and Alexander found themselves navigating a treacherous landscape of deception and manipulation, where loyalties were tested at every turn.

Amidst the chaos, Sarah and Alexander's bond deepened. The weight of their shared mission, the adrenaline-fueled highs, and the heart-wrenching lows forged a connection that defied the boundaries of their predetermined roles. They found solace in each other's presence, a beacon of strength in a world shrouded in darkness. But their burgeoning romance was a double-edged sword. It brought them joy and comfort in the face of adversity, yet it also exposed them to vulnerability. Maelstrom exploited their emotions, using them as leverage to weaken their resolve and drive a wedge between them. Sarah and Alexander knew they had to remain vigilant, their hearts shielded as they worked tirelessly to dismantle Maelstrom. The fate of nations rested on their shoulders, and they would not let personal desires compromise their mission.

As the team closed in on Maelstrom's inner circle, they realized the true extent of the enemy's power. The battle they were waging was not just against a single organization; it was a fight against corruption and greed that permeated the very fabric of society. In the heart-stopping moments leading up to their final assault, Sarah and Alexander steeled themselves for the ultimate confrontation. The lines between friend and foe blurred, and they knew that sacrifices would have to be made. They were prepared to risk everything—their lives, their love, and the fragile world they were fighting to protect. With their team standing united, fueled by a shared purpose and an unbreakable spirit, Sarah and Alexander prepared to confront Maelstrom head-on. The stage was set for a battle that would determine the course of history and shape the destiny of nations.

Chapter 7

Shadows Collide

"What's the update?" Alexander asked Mia, who was working e inches from the screen of her laptop. Mia was a former IT expert in the Russian FSB. She oversaw cyber operations in the agency such as the 2016 election meddling in the US. After the invasion of Ukraine, the Russian government downsized the cyber wing of the various intelligence agencies and Mia was one of the unlucky ones. Since then, she had developed a grudge against the Russians. She felt betrayed.

"Maelstrom. This is it." She turned the laptop toward Alex, who had sat down, keeping his coffee mug on the table. The screen on Mia's MacBook showed a document. Alex pulled the laptop toward him. It was a manifesto.

The Newest World Order: Maelstrom

In a world riddled with chaos and inequity, Maelstrom rises as a beacon of change. We stand united, driven by a relentless pursuit of power and order. Our aim is to dismantle the oppressive machinery of governments that breed corruption and stagnation, ushering in an era of true dominance.

We reject the status quo, advocating for a new world order under our unwavering control. With strategic prowess, we harness technology, resources, and strategic alliances to shatter the chains of existing power structures. The old must crumble to make way for the new, and Maelstrom shall reign supreme.

Unapologetically audacious, we embrace disruption as a means to an end. Our actions are fueled by the conviction that only through chaos can true order emerge. We commandeer the chaos, sculpting it into a weapon to dismantle nations, dissolve borders, and rewrite history as we see fit.

Yet, we are not merely conquerors; we are visionaries. We promise a world governed by our benevolent rule, where innovation flourishes, resources are optimized, and society thrives under our guidance. Maelstrom's legacy is one of dominance, progress, and a testament to the indomitable will of those who dare to reshape the world in their image.

"Damn. How'd you get this?" Alex looked at Mia.

"I'm just resourceful like that," Mia replied.

"That you are, Miss Mia Egorov." Alex smiled. "Hey Sarah, come here. Look at this shit."

"I have something else too," Mia said as Sarah read the Maelstrom manifesto with wide eyes.

"Hmmmm?" Alex looked at Mia. She pointed toward the laptop.

"You wanna show me you MacBook?" Alex laughed.

"What the fuck?" Sarah looked up at Alex.

"Exactly. They want to take over the world. Sounds like a plot for some low budget political thriller." Alex chuckled. Mia pressed some keys on the laptop and turned it toward Alex and Sarah once again. It was a live stream of a large compound. There were guards patrolling the huge walls and the gate was protected by soldiers that seemed to belong to some Special Forces.

"What's this?" Sarah asked.

"It's a Maelstrom compound in the outskirts of Budapest," Mia replied.

"What's inside?" Alex interjected.

"I don't know. I couldn't access the cameras inside the building. Maybe there are none." Mia seemed annoyed. She did not like it when she was unable to do something even if it was outside her control.

"We have to know," Sarah said sternly.

"How do you plan to get inside?" Mia asked. "Even if you do sneak past the guards, which is impossible by the way, you can't hide from the cameras."

Alex and Sarah went silent. They stared at the screen as several thoughts rushed into their minds. After a few seconds, Sarah spoke.

"What's that?" She asked, pointing toward the laptop. Mia zoomed in. A vehicle approached the gate and immediately entered into the compound.

"This vehicle comes in everyday several times over," Mia said. "It comes at night as well."

"How do you know that?" Alex asked.

"I've been watching this feed since a week," Mia answered.

"A week? Why didn't you tell us before?"

"I wasn't sure if this was Maelstrom only. I had asked a contact in Russia to confirm. He just got back to me a while back."

"Zoom in on it," Sarah instructed Mia. It was a black Suzuki Vitara with a registration plate that seemed bogus. Sarah smiled.

"I'm gonna go use the restroom real quick," Mia said.

"What are you thinking?" Alex asked, looking at Sarah.

"This might seem crazy, but it's doable." Sarah was still smiling.

"What exactly, Sarah?"

"We locate this car. We take the driver hostage, and drive into the compound. That's the only way in."

"Hold up. So many things could go wrong there," Alex exclaimed.

"Like what?"

"For starters, what if there are armed guards in the car? How are we going to take down Maelstrom if we're dead? And what if they stop us at the gate? What then?" Alex asked.

"We have to take that risk, Alex." Sarah looked determined. "It's going to work, trust me." She held Alex's hand in hers. They locked eyes with each other for a few seconds. Both of them felt a strong connection. Sarah leaned in and kissed him. Her hand was gripping his palm. They stared at each other for a few more seconds before Mia walked in.

"Oh, I'm sorry." Mia looked visibly awkward.

"Relax. Nothing happening," Alex chuckled. Sarah blushed and looked outside the small window that overlooked the street. Alex told her about Sarah's plan.

"There are no armed guards in the car. It's just Xavier Malcom and his driver," Mia casually said.

"Wait, what? Did you say Xavier Malcolm?" Sarah almost shouted.

"Jeez, relax. Yes, Xavier Malcolm."

"You mean the head of Maelstrom?" Alex asked.

"Yeah."

"Okay, this is great. What else do you know about him or his routine?"

"He's a paranoid guy. That's all I know. This is why he's sends his car to different places while he's in the compound the entire time. He wants people to think he's always on the go." Alex and Sarah looked puzzled. "Yeah, I don't get it either," Mia said.

"How armed is he? Any idea?" Sarah asked.

"Not much. A pistol, maybe. Not more than that."

Sarah and Alexander looked at each other.

"Call Frank. Give him the details of the car and tell him to keep an eye on it," Sarah instructed Mia.

Frank Szabo was one of their best resources in Hungary. He was an ex-Információs Hivatal agent who had served for almost twenty five years. He was abandoned by the Hungarian government on a clandestine mission in Uzbekistan. He had been working as a Private Investigator since then until Alex employed him through a local Hungarian contact.

"The next train leaves in three hours," Sarah said.

"Let's go."

***

It was 1am when they got out at a station in Budapest. The chilly December air felt crisp as Sarah and Alexander stepped out of the train. Sarah was dressed all black. She had a hoodie on that had a teddy bear printed on it. Her hazel colored eyes shone bright under the station lights. Alex paused for a second as he stared at her.

"Hello?" Sarah snapped her fingers in front of his eyes. "Are you okay?" The blushing in her cheeks showed that she knew Alex was locked in on her.

"Yeah, I'm good," Alex looked down and let out a slight giggle. "We're fifteen minutes away from Frank's place." They stopped a cab and got inside.

"I'm gonna take a quick nap," Sarah said, closing her eyes. She snuggled up to Alex as he put an arm around her. He smiled to himself and closed his eyes.

The cab stopped right outside Frank's house about twenty minutes later. They stepped out and went inside. Frank was expecting them.

"Hello, my friends," he greeted them enthusiastically in his Hungarian accent. Frank led them into a small room.

"Did you find it?" Alex asked.

"The car leaves 5am in the morning from St. Stephen's Basilica. It stops at the compound. Doesn't stop anywhere else," Frank said, impressed with his homework.

"Alright, you know the plan?" Sarah asked.

"Of course," Frank replied.

The next morning Sarah and Alex reached St. Stephen's Basilica. Alex glanced at watch. I was 4:49. There was no sign of the car. They waited for a couple of minutes before Sarah spotted a black Suzuki Vitara stopping right at the entrance. It seemed as if it was waiting for someone.

Alex sneaked up from behind and opened the door. He punched the driver, knocking him unconscious. Alex signaled Sarah who ran up to him. They picked him the unconscious driver and put him in the trunk. Alex took the wheel and Sarah hid in the trunk. A few minutes later, Alex saw a bald man approaching the car. He had his sunglasses on and he was clad in black tuxedo. He had a vape in one hand and a briefcase in the other.

"Xavier Malcolm," Alex said under his breath.

As soon as he sat in the car, he knew something was not right.

"Drive," he said in Hungarian. When Alex did not respond, Xavier looked at him in the rear view mirror. Immediately, he knew it was not his driver. Before he could do anything, Sarah put a gun to his head from behind.

"Don't move, asshole," she yelled. As Alex put the car in drive, Sarah knocked Xavier out too. She duck taped the two men and climbed into the front seat. Alex put up his hand. His fingers were crossed. Sarah kissed his hand. They both knew it was a 'do or die' mission.

"Mia, you there?" Sarah spoke into her earpiece.

"Present."

"Frank?"

"*Itt.*"

"Theo, Markus , and Luke?"

"Right behind you," Luke answered. The three men were in a black sedan following them from a distance. They were retired Blackwater operatives who were good friends with Alex. He had gotten them on the team from the very start.

"Remember, you guys stop five kilometers from the compound, alright?" Sarah confirmed the plan.

"Yes, ma'am," Theo replied.

Sarah and Alexander stood at the precipice of the final battle, the weight of their mission pressing heavily upon them. The time for covert operations and subtle maneuvers had passed. It was time to confront Maelstrom head-on and expose their insidious plans to the world. Their team, a formidable force united by a common purpose, prepared for the assault on Maelstrom's secret stronghold. Each member had honed their skills, knowing that failure would have dire consequences not only for themselves but for countless innocent lives. As they approached the heavily guarded compound, tension hung in the air like a heavy fog.

The team moved with precision and stealth, exploiting weaknesses in the enemy's defenses.

Sarah and Alexander reached inside the compound with ease. The guards at the gate let them through, oblivious to who was sitting inside those tinted windows. Once inside, they counted the men who were keeping watch. There were hardly fifteen men outside. The compound inside was empty. They looked at each other, a sense of determination in their eyes. Sarah took out her Glock and put on a suppressor. Alex followed suit. They took out the men at the front gate with relative ease.

"Two down, you're clear to attack," Sarah radioed the three men. It barely took them ten minutes before crashing in and opening fire on the remaining guards. Alexander and Sarah led the charge, their unwavering resolve inspiring those around them. The clash between the resistance fighters and Maelstrom's forces was fierce and relentless. Bullets flew, explosions rocked the compound, and the sound of combat echoed through the corridors. Sarah and Alexander fought side by side, their movements synchronized as if they were a single entity. Their connection, both on a personal and professional level, elevated their combat prowess. Sarah's mind raced, searching for the key to unraveling Maelstrom's intricate web of deception. She had seen glimpses of their true intentions, but the whole picture remained elusive. The battle was not only physical but also intellectual—a chess game of strategy and manipulation.

With each enemy they defeated, Sarah and Alexander gathered fragments of information, piecing together the puzzle that had haunted them since the beginning. Maelstrom's operations spanned borders, infiltrating governments, finance, and technology sectors. It was a well-oiled machine, driven by the insatiable thirst for power and control. As they neared the heart of the compound, Sarah's instincts guided her towards a hidden vault—the repository of Maelstrom's darkest secrets. She knew that within its impenetrable walls lay the answers they sought, the evidence that would expose Maelstrom's true nature to the world.

Breathing heavily, sweat dripping down her brow, Sarah skillfully picked the vault's lock. The door swung open, revealing a room lined with files, hard drives, and classified documents. She and Alexander began scouring the contents, searching for the final piece of the puzzle. Theo, Luke and Markus stood at the gates as their bosses went through the files.

"Make it quick, I don't want more of these assholes to show up," Markus shouted.

As they delved deeper into the vault's secrets, a chilling truth emerged. Maelstrom's ultimate goal was not just control or power; it was to destabilize entire regions, to sow chaos and discord on a global scale. They manipulated governments, incited conflicts, and orchestrated acts of terror—all to further their sinister agenda.

The realization sent shockwaves through Sarah and Alexander, fueling their determination to expose Maelstrom's crimes. With the evidence in their possession, they knew they had to escape the compound and bring the truth to light. But Maelstrom wasn't ready to relinquish its grip on power.

As the two of them made their way back through the compound, a team of Maelstrom soldiers arrived at the gate. Some of them even dropped from above. The final battle raged around them as they fought their way back through the compound's labyrinthine corridors. The enemy, desperate to protect their secrets, launched a relentless assault, determined to eliminate anyone who stood in their way. Sarah and Alexander's team fought valiantly, their resolve unyielding in the face of overwhelming odds. With each step they took, they moved closer to the compound's exit, closer to the outside world where the truth could no longer be silenced.

As explosions rocked the compound and gunfire filled the air, Sarah and Alexander emerged from the shadows, carrying the weight of the truth on their shoulders. They had survived the onslaught, but their journey was far from over. As they regrouped with their team, battered but victorious, Sarah and Alexander knew that their fight had only just begun. Maelstrom may have been weakened, but its tendrils extended far and wide. It was up to them to expose the truth, to dismantle the organization, and to ensure that justice prevailed. United by a shared purpose and an unbreakable bond, they looked towards the horizon, ready to face the challenges that lay ahead. The world would never be the same, but Sarah and Alexander were determined to shape its future for the better.

"What about Xavier?" Alex asked.

"Where is he?" Luke interjected before Sarah could respond.

"In the car." Alex pointed to the compound.

"The black Suzuki Vitara?" Luke asked.

"Yeah."

"Let's just say Xavier isn't around anymore," Markus chuckled.

"What do you mean?" Sarah asked.

"The Maelstrom soldiers. They riddled the car with bullets when we were hiding behind it. I thought you guys had taken him inside with you," Theo said.

"Ah, fuck it. The world wouldn't miss the bastard." Alex replied.

As they turned toward the exit, a bullet hit Theo in the leg. They turned around to find Xavier firing from behind the car. Alex and Sarah quickly hid behind a pillar as Luke and Markus dragged an injured Theo to safety.

"Where are you hit?" Markus asked.

"Don't worry. It's just a flesh wound." Theo pulled up his pants to reveal a wound in his calf. "Go, get that asshole," Theo said.

By the time Markus and Luke went out, Xavier was already in handcuffs. Alex pushed him as Xavier looked at Sarah with rage in his eyes.

"Idiots. You think you can get away with this? I'm gonna fuck you up. Each and every one of you motherfuckers. You wanna save yourselves? Kill me right now. Leaving me alive would be the biggest mistake. I will hunt you down," Xavier said. His voice seemed firm and crisp. Markus felt goosebumps on his arms. There was something about Xavier that was terrifying.

"Sure, asshole," Alex said sarcastically.

Markus and Luke lifted Theo and put him in the car.

"Take him with you. Meet us at the embassy," Alex instructed.

Alex and Sarah stole a separate car from the compound. Alex stared at Sarah as she tried to hotwire the car. There was a glimmer in his eyes.

In a world of shadows and secrets, love and duty had intertwined, creating a force that could topple empires and change the course of history. As they walked into the unknown, hand in hand, their hearts filled with hope, for they knew that even in the darkest of times, the light would always find a way to break through.

Chapter 8

The Unveiling

The room was cloaked in an air of tension as Sarah and Alexander stood before a packed auditorium, ready to reveal the truth they had fought so hard to uncover. Cameras flashed, journalists scribbled furiously on their notepads, and anticipation hung heavy in the air. The stage was set for the most crucial moment of their lives—the public unveiling of Maelstrom's sinister operations. The evidence they had amassed, the connections they had unraveled, and the sacrifices they had made had all led to this pivotal moment.

Sarah stepped forward, her voice steady and resolute. "Ladies and gentlemen, esteemed guests, today we stand before you to expose the true face of corruption. We're here to uncover an organization that extremely close to disrupting the world order. We think that the biggest threat to humankind is nuclear weapons or information warfare. We never thought it would be an organization seeking to overthrow governments. Maelstrom, a clandestine terrorist organization of power and manipulation, has been operating in the shadows, pulling the strings of governments, economies, and lives." A hush fell over the audience, the weight of Sarah's words sinking in. There were some subtle murmurs here and there. Sarah looked around before continuing. She could sense the anxiousness in the room. As she took a sip from the glass in front of her, Alex looked at her and smiled. The crowd was too focused on Sarah to notice Alex. She continued, her voice filled with conviction. "Their actions have caused immeasurable harm, instigated conflicts, and perpetuated suffering. But no more. Today, we bring their dark deeds into the light, where they can no longer hide. Alex?" Sarah looked at him.

"Thank you, Sarah," Alex began. He adjusted the mic to his level. "As Sarah said, Maelstrom had contributed directly or indirectly to every global conflict that has taken place over the last few decades. We have evidence that it was Maelstrom that enabled Kim to constantly develop nuclear weapons. We also have proof of the organization meddling in US elections and even in the White House. No one was safe. We do not have conclusive evidence as of now whether Xavier Malcolm, the CEO of Maelstrom has the Kremlin's backing. But we'll get to the bottom of it." Alex paused. The mention of Russia had made the presser even more interesting.

"You're saying that Maelstrom is the brainchild of the Kremlin?" A reporter in the second row asked.

"Yes. Maelstrom was a program initiated in the Soviet Union. We have evidence that this was a continuation of the program. The idea was the same. Whether it has links to the Russian government or not is yet to be established. Let me show you some of the documents we recovered from the compound in Budapest." Alex signaled Sarah to switch on the screens behind her.

Images and documents appeared on the giant screens, revealing the inner workings of Maelstrom. The audience gasped as they saw the faces of politicians, corporate moguls, and influential figures implicated in Maelstrom's schemes. The screen showed the inside of Maelstrom's compounds all around the world. There were torture cells and interrogation rooms in every one of them. The pictures and documents also showed high profile politicians taking bribes from Maelstrom to advance the organization's agenda.

Alexander joined Sarah on the stage, his gaze steady and determined. He knew he couldn't have achieved this without the support of Sarah. Her resilience and consistency had helped them bring down Maelstrom. Sarah looked at Alex.

"Can you believe it? We just took down the most evil organization in history. For too long, this network of shadowy figures has manipulated the world stage for their agenda. And you know, we have the power to change that. We've already decimated their operation. We can dismantle Maelstrom fully. And bring justice to those who have suffered under its reign," Alex said. Sarah gave him a determined nod. She knew they had to complete what they had started.

As Sarah and Alexander presented their evidence, the room erupted in a mix of disbelief, anger, and determination. The reporters could not compute what they were being shown. They needed more details but they did not know where to start from.

"Marie from the New York Times." A reporter raised her hand. "You're saying that a conspiracy this big was occurring since years and not one intelligence agency knew about it? They're that incompetent?" She sounded angry.

"Not really. It was actually a joint operation between the CIA and MI6," Alex said, pointing toward Sarah.

"It took two of the world's best intelligence agencies decades to uncover a global conspiracy?" The reporter fired in another question.

"One question per person, please," Sarah interjected. They did not know how to tackle these questions. They were field agents, not PR personnel. The two answered a few more questions before deciding it was too much for them.

Members of the audience whispered in disbelief at the scale of the conspiracy they had just witnessed. It was just incomprehensible.

Outside the walls of the auditorium, the public's hunger for truth was insatiable. Before the presser was over, there were already calls for mass protests by various groups that called for better security measures. The revelations sparked a wildfire of outrage that quickly spread across social media and news outlets. People from all corners of the world demanded action, calling for investigations and accountability.

But as the public's attention focused on their cause, Sarah and Alexander knew the battle was far from over. Maelstrom would not go down without a fight. They knew Xavier Malcolm would strike back. They did not know how or when but they were sure of it. Their enemies lurked in the shadows, plotting their next move, and determined to silence those who threatened their existence.

A few minutes later, Alex and Sarah left the auditorium for their temporary headquarters. Alex let out a huge sigh as soon as he sat inside. Sarah chuckled. Before they could discuss what just happened, Alex's phone rang. It was David.

"Hi, there!" Alex said casually.

"What the fuck, Davis?" David shouted.

"Woah, relax buddy."

"Don't tell me to fucking relax. You've been running an undercover op since four months? Using the agency's resources? What is happening?" David was livid.

"I can explain," Alex muttered.

"Don't. Do you have any idea what this does to us? Our reputation? No one, in a million years, is gonna trust the CIA. You just annihilated our legacy. You're done. You are to report to station immediately," David instructed. Before Alex could respond, David cut the call.

"What happened?" Sarah asked. She could hear David shout from the other end but could not figure out what he had said.

"Ummm, I think I just got fired from the CIA." Alex chuckled. "You didn't get a call?"

"I retired from MI6 a month ago. I doubt I'll get a call," Sarah responded.

"What? Why didn't you tell me?"

"I didn't want to distract you, or anyone else on the team."

Alex went quiet for moment.

"Fuck, I said in the presser that this was a joint operation."

"It's fine. No one really cares about MI6 when the CIA is involved," Sarah laughed.

They reached their apartment a few minutes later. They had gotten used to the narrow streets of Prague. Sarah and Alexander convened with their team. The air crackled with urgency and tension as they discussed their next steps. They knew they had to stay one step ahead, to outsmart and outmaneuver their adversaries.

Sarah's voice cut through the room, her eyes shining with determination. "We need to continue gathering evidence, build alliances, and protect ourselves. We cannot let our guard down. Maelstrom will stop at nothing to protect their interests."

"We must be prepared for whatever comes our way. And we don't even have the backing of our agencies anymore. I just got laid off and Sarah retired. That doesn't mean we can't pull it off. Expect some turbulence. We not only have to get Maelstrom, we have to do it quick. If the CIA gets to them first, I don't know how it'll pan out. Maelstrom has people within the CIA. We've come this far, and we owe it to the people whose lives have been affected by Maelstrom's actions. We will not rest until justice is served." Alexander's voice was filled with conviction.

***

Days turned into nights, and the battle against Maelstrom intensified. Sarah and Alexander expanded their team. They moved like shadows, uncovering more layers of the intricate web that the organization had woven. The more they dived in, the more messed up it became. At some points, it seemed impossible to finish off Maelstrom but they knew they had to go on. It wasn't just Maelstrom they were taking on. There were other powerful people. Politicians, Generals, Judges, Businessmen, and others were involved.

They gathered testimonies, exposed hidden accounts, and connected the dots, piece by piece. With each revelation, their resolve grew stronger. They understood the risks involved, and the dangers they faced, but the pursuit of justice fueled their determination. The world was watching, waiting for their next move, and Sarah and Alexander were determined to deliver.

Chapter 9

Shadows of Betrayal

Alex entered the ten-storied building covered in blue glass in the diplomatic enclave in Vienna. The air inside the building smelled like lavender.

That's odd for a building that hosts the CIA.

He walked into the lobby in his crisp black suit with a white shirt and a blue tie. His hair was gelled back, and his Rolex Submariner shone beneath the lights. Alex sat on a sofa and waited. He tapped his heels anxiously as he waited for someone to receive him. It reminded him of the US embassy building in London. He smiled to himself at the thought of him being there.

A few minutes had gone by when David walked in. His face showed no expressions, although Alexander knew what he was thinking. David nodded at him.

"Wow, not even a *hello*?" Alex asked as he stood up and followed David.

"It took you six months to fuck this up. When you were assigned this case in London, they thought you'd mess it up within the first three. That's an achievement," David said as he walked firmly. Alex chuckled.

They entered the Chief of Station's room. He was already at his table. He looked up and asked them both to sit. After two minutes, he greeted them and opened his laptop.

"Deputy Director Bishop is going to be joining us," he said.

David could see Alex looking at him from the corner of his eye, but he chose not to make eye contact. He just stared at the COS.

"Deputy Director," the COS exclaimed. "I have David Blair and Alexander Davis with me." He turned the laptop around.

"David, Alex. Let's get straight to the point. Your little show in Prague hasn't set well with Langley." She paused for a second. "No one's said it out loud, but they consider it treason. Now, I can make sure no one uses the T-word here, and no one follows through on it, but you both are done," Bishop said.

"Ma'am, I just-"

"Thank you, take care." Bishop disconnected the call before David could complete his sentence. He looked at Alex with rage.

"Thank you, gentlemen," the COS said as he got busy on his laptop. David and Alex left the building together and sat in Alex's car.

"Listen, I can-"

"Save it. What are you guys doing? What all do you know? Do you have a better chance at getting Maelstrom than the CIA?" David fired a series of questions at Alex. Alex smiled. He knew where David was getting to.

"Definitely. The CIA doesn't know shit. They don't have the kind of resources we have. And they definitely don't have a way to tell if there are Maelstrom agents within the agency," Alex replied plainly.

David thought for a while, his eyes staring at the street lamp right in front of the hood.

"Take me in," he said. Alex smiled once again and started the car. As they left the parking lot, Alex's phone rang. It was Sarah.

***

Sarah and Alexander knew that their fight against Maelstrom would not be without its treachery and betrayal. As they delved deeper into the heart of the conspiracy, the lines between friend and foe blurred, and the trust they had placed in specific individuals were put to the test.

The same evening, as the team gathered in their safe house, tension hung thick in the air. Sarah's gaze shifted uneasily between the faces of her comrades, searching for any signs of deception. A sense of unease gripped her heart, an instinctual warning that danger lurked within their midst. Alex still hadn't told her about their new recruit.

She turned to Alexander, her voice filled with concern. "Something's not right. I can feel it. We must remain vigilant. Our enemies are cunning, and they won't hesitate to exploit any weakness."

Alexander nodded, his eyes scanning the room. "I sense it too. We've grown complacent, too trusting. It's time to reassess our allegiances and ensure that our circle remains untainted." He paused for a moment. "David, my RA."

"Yeah, what about him?" Sarah asked.

"He's on the team."

"What do you mean he's on the team? He's CIA. How can he be 'on the team?' And when did that happen?"

"Relax," Alex said. "He also got fired from the agency. He wants in now. He's a brilliant resource. I don't wanna lose him. Trust me." Alex stared at Sarah for a full minute. She stared back. He pulled her away from the team and held her against the wall. He leaned in to kiss her. Their passionate kiss made them forget about all the worry in the world. They went back outside after a few minutes.

"I haven't officially inducted him, but I will, and he knows that," Alex said. He highlighted David's achievements. Sarah nodded.

"Let's just wait for a few days. I want to monitor the team before we bring in someone new," Sarah responded.

Two days had passed. Sarah and Alexander were sitting in the safe house having a drink when Luke came in running. He seemed shaken.

"What's up?" Alex asked casually.

"It's Markus," he said in a low voice.

"What about him?" Sarah kept her mug on the table.

"He's gone."

"What do you mean gone?"

"Theo and I have been calling him since yesterday morning. He's gone."

"Son of a bitch, I knew it," Sarah yelled.

"Relax. Let's not jump to conclusions. What if someone picked him up?"

"No one picked him up," Luke interjected. "He packed his stuff and disappeared. We checked the CCTVs. He sat in a white Toyota Corolla and vanished. Switched his phone, his GPS, everything."

"Fucking hell. Of all the people, it was Markus," Alex laughed to himself.

"We need to find out where Markus went," Sarah looked at Alex.

"What do you mean where Markus went? Of course, he went to Mael. Where else would he go?" Alex sounded disappointed but not worried.

"With the kind of intel he has, he can take our entire operation down," Sarah said.

"We need to change this place. Right now!" Alex got up and hurried into the next room where everyone else was sitting. "You all know about Markus. Before anything else, it's important that we change the location of our safe house. Pack up. You have three hours." He walked back into Sarah's room.

"Where are we gonna go?" Sarah asked. He ignored her question as he picked up his phone and dialed.

"Dave, hey. We've got a problem. Yeah, we need a place. A new HQ. We're around eleven people. Yeah, okay. Sounds good. We're on our way." Alex hung up. "David has a place. In the suburbs."

Alex and Sarah knew they were in danger. Not only theirs but their entire team's safety was at stake. Sarah looked at Alex as he drove through the streets of Prague in the dead of night.

"We need to follow that bastard," she said in a low voice.

"Damn right, we do. We need to be careful, though."

***

"Mia, do we have something?" Sarah asked, hours after they settled down in the new place. Mia was glued to her laptop screen.

"Yes, actually." She turned the laptop toward her. "He's here." She pointed to a red circle on a city map.

"France?" Sarah asked.

"Yes, Normandy. This warehouse." Mia tapped her finger on the screen.

"How do you know?" Alex asked.

Mia pointed toward Alan. Alan was their most resourceful asset when it came to Europe. He, too, was a former MI6 operative. Alan knew every bit of Europe like the back of his hand. He had contacts in every corner of the continent.

"One of my guys in France told me that a guy matching Markus's description got off a train. He followed him to Normandy at this warehouse."

"Good work, Markus."

"A word?" Sarah asked Alex. They stepped out of the room and into the small balcony. "When are we leaving?" She asked.

"Right now," Alex replied. The determination in both of their voices was unmatched. "We need to get to the bottom of this. What's our game plan?"

"We go in, locate Markus, and extract him," Sarah said.

"What if it's not that simple? What if the place is crawling with Maelstrom soldiers?" Alex asked.

"Then we'll just do our thing," Sarah replied. As Alex turned to go back inside, Sarah caught hold of his arm and kissed him.

***

Alex and Sarah reached Caen the next morning. After traveling for almost two hours, they spotted the warehouse from a distance. It was the only building for miles. Alex looked at Sarah.

"This is it," he said. Sarah nodded.

"We're going in," she spoke in her earpiece. "Mia, what do you have for us?"

"The security is too much right now. There's a supply door at the backside. You guys can get in from there undetected."

A few minutes later, they stopped their car behind.

"We'll have to walk from here," Sarah said. They got out of the car and reached the back of the warehouse undetected. Alex picked the lock, and they entered inside. As they stepped inside, Sarah's earpiece produced static before going dead.

"Shit, they probably have some kind of jammers," she whispered. Alex instructed her to focus on their mission.

With caution and weapons at the ready, Sarah and Alexander crept through the dimly lit corridors of the warehouse. The distant sound of voices sent a chill down their spines, their hearts pounding in their chests.

As they approached an open door, their senses heightened. They witnessed a scene that left them speechless. Markus stood in the center of a circle, surrounded by a group of individuals clad in black, their faces masked by shadows. It was clear that he had been playing a double game—a pawn in Maelstrom's intricate chessboard. Sarah's voice broke through the silence, laced with a mix of anger and betrayal. "Markus, how could you? We trusted you."

Markus met their gazes, his face a mixture of remorse and desperation. "I'm sorry. They kidnapped my family. I had no choice."

"There's always a choice, Markus. We could have protected you and your family. We could have fought this together." Sarah's voice softened, her eyes filled with empathy.

But it was too late to apologize. The sound of footsteps echoed in the distance, signaling the arrival of more soldiers. The betrayal had been exposed, and Sarah and Alexander found themselves in a dangerous situation. A fierce battle erupted within the warehouse as Sarah and Alexander fought to defend themselves against Markus and Maelstrom's enforcers. Their survival instincts kicked into overdrive, and their training and skills tested to their limits.

As the battle raged on, Sarah and Alexander found themselves back-to-back, their movements synchronized as they fended off their attackers. Their trust in each other, forged through shared experiences and a love that had weathered countless storms, gave them strength. With every soldier they killed, the truth became more apparent. Maelstrom's influence had penetrated deeper than they had ever imagined. The enemies they faced were not just faceless agents but friends and allies corrupted by the allure of power and self-preservation.

As the final soldier fell, Sarah and Alexander stood amidst the wreckage, their bodies bruised and battered but their spirits unyielding. They knew that the battle against Maelstrom had taken a dangerous turn. The web of deception had ensnared those closest to them, and the price of trust had been steep. But they refused to be broken.

Alex walked over to Markus's body. He looked at it with disgust as Sarah watched from the other end of the room, surrounded by bodies. The revelation of betrayal only fueled their determination to expose Maelstrom's true face and dismantle its operations once and for all.

"Let's go, Alex," she said.

As they walked out of the warehouse, Sarah's phone rang. It was Mia. She answered it immediately.

"What?" Sarah held the phone to her ear for a few seconds before she yelled. She dropped the phone from her hand.

Chapter 10

Redemption's Call

Sarah tried to compose herself. She put the phone in her pocket and stared into the distance. It was as if she was drowning in regret.

"What happened?" Alex asked.

"Markus was on our side," Sarah said.

"What do you mean?"

"They found a note under his mattress. He was just pretending to be with Maelstrom. Would've gotten out on the first opportunity as soon as his family was safe." Sarah fell silent for a minute. "God damnit!" She shouted.

"Relax. You didn't know. No one did," Alex consoled her.

"I wanted to believe he was dirty. I should've dug in deeper."

"If Markus wasn't dirty, it doesn't mean no one else will be. We have to be careful. We had information, we acted upon it. It made sense at the time. That's it. Don't worry about it."

Sarah was amazed at how calm and composed Alex was.

"He has two little children, Alex." It seemed like Sarah would break down.

"And we'll take care of them like our own. When we hire these people, they know what they're getting into. This is not on us," Alex reassured her.

"I shot him in the head. How am I supposed to live with that?" Sarah asked.

Alex stayed silent. The two walked back to their car and rode in silence until Alex spoke.

"We can't go back to Prague. They know how we look like. We can't put any more of our people in danger," Alex said, looking at the road.

"What do you have in mind?" Sarah looked at him. Alex took a moment to think.

"I know a guy in Kherson. Keeps a low profile. We'll be safe there."

"Kherson?" Sarah exclaimed. Alex nodded.

An hour into the drive, Sarah took her phone from her pocket. She was still shaken from what had happened at the warehouse. She dialed Luke.

"Where are you guys? Your comms went dead. So did your phones. We were worried sick." Theo almost yelled.

"Relax. We're fine. We're on our way to somewhere safe. It's not safe for you if we're at the safe house," Sarah explained.

"What do you mean? Someplace safe? Where exactly?" Luke probed. Alex signaled Sarah to not tell him.

"You're breaking up, Luke. I'll call you when we get there. Bye." She cut the call. "Why aren't we telling them? I trust every single person in the headquarters in Prague."

"There's no need to tell anyone plus our phones might be tapped, who knows? We have to be careful," Alex replied. "Also, you should get some sleep. It's a long way to Kherson."

Sarah leaned in and gave Alex a peck on the cheek before leaning back on her seat.

***

"They've eliminated Markus," Luke said, speaking on the phone.

"I know that. Where are they now?"

"I'm not sure. They wouldn't tell me. Morgan said they're going someplace safe. I have no idea where they're going."

"Alright, let me handle it."

Luke walked back inside the safe house. All of them seemed indulged in work in one way or the other, trying to bring down Maelstrom and making sure that Sarah and Alex are kept safe. Little did they know that they had a mole amongst them. Luke looked at them as a million thoughts ran through his mind. He had been hired by Xavier himself three years back. When Maelstrom found out about Alex and Sarah's efforts against them, they sent in Luke as a counter measure.

***

In the aftermath of the warehouse battle, Sarah and Alexander retreated to a secluded hideaway in Kherson—a place where they could regroup, heal their wounds, and devise a new strategy. The fear of betrayal lingered in their hearts, but they knew they couldn't afford to dwell on it. The fight against Maelstrom demanded their unwavering focus and determination.

They reached Kherson after travelling for about a day and a half. The city of Kherson had been ruined because of the war. The buildings were never reconstructed and it still looked like a warzone.

"Do you know where it is?" Sarah asked. The exhaustion on both of their faces was apparent.

"Yeah, we're five minutes away." Alex looked at his phone.

They pulled up to a shabby looking building in a desolate area away from the city. The street looked empty apart from the few stray dogs roaming around. There was a house on the far end of the street that had a light on.

"This is it," Alex said, turning off the engine. "Fourth floor. He says it's not locked."

"What is this place?" Sarah looked around at the post-apocalyptic setting around her. "Does anyone even live in this building?" She asked.

"No, it's empty. Been like that since years," Alex casually answered. They stepped inside the rusted gate and turned on the flashlights on their phones. The bulb on the entrance was fused.

"We're gonna have to use the stairs," Alex said. "There's no elevators here."

"Yeah, no shit. You think I would have gotten into an elevator in this building?" Sarah chuckled.

As they made their way up the dark staircase, Alex noticed graffiti on the walls.

"It looks like a Soviet era establishment, look." He pointed toward a particular wall. It had a hammer and sickle spray painted on it with the words 'Да здравствует Брежнев!'

"What does that mean?" Sarah asked.

"Long Live Brezhnev!" Alex smiled. "Let's go."

The two reached the top floor. It only had one apartment. Alex picked the lock and they entered inside. He flicked open a switch, which illuminated the entire apartment.

It was fully carpeted and seemed like it had just been cleaned. The walls inside were clean and without cracks. In fact, the air inside the apartment smelled crisp and fresh. The lighting itself was comprehensive.

"I could get used to this," Sarah remarked. "I wasn't expecting this, giving the state of the rest of the building."

"He gave me a heads up. It's his regular safe house. And it makes sense. I mean no one would look for anyone here," Alex responded.

Before Alex could look around any further, Sarah pushed and against the wall and kissed him. Alex wrapped his arms around her as his hands ran through her hair. The two forgot how exhausted they were as they pushed their bodies against each other's. Alex took her hand and led her to a room. He threw her on the bed as both of them undressed.

***

The next morning, Sarah woke up to an empty bed. She lay in bed for a few minutes, reminiscing the previous night. She could hear Alex in the kitchen.

"What are you doing?"

"Making us breakfast. What do you want?"

"What do we have?"

Alex laughed.

"Eggs."

"And?"

"That's about it," Alex responded.

"In that case, I'll have some scrambled eggs."

Alex threw himself on the sofa after breakfast. Sarah joined him after a while. They both sat in silence, knowing what the other person was thinking.

"I just-"

"Last night-"

They both spoke at the same time.

"You go first," Alex said.

"I was just saying that last night was nice." Sarah blushed.

"I was going to say the same." Alex smiled at her. "But Sarah, we can't let ourselves get distracted."

"We clearly have a thing for each other, Alex. And I don't think I have ever felt something this strongly for anyone. I know how risky it is. The things we do. But I just can't help it."

Alex leaned in and kissed her.

"I'm glad we're on this mission together. There's no one else I'd rather be with."

Sarah smiled.

"Let's take a look at what we gathered from the warehouse," Alex said, reaching for his bag.

"Yeah."

As they surveyed the evidence, it became clear that Maelstrom's web of deception extended far beyond what they had initially imagined. It had infiltrated governments, corporations, and even influential individuals within their ranks. Their task seemed daunting, but they were fueled by a renewed sense of purpose. There was a glimmer of determination in their eyes.

"We might have faced setbacks but we cannot allow ourselves to be defeated. The truth must prevail, and we will not rest until Maelstrom's dark grip on the world is shattered. We must be vigilant, not only against external threats but also against the insidious nature of betrayal." Sarah said, her voice filled with excitement and conviction.

Alex nodded in agreement, his determination shining in his eyes. They understood the gravity of their mission and the sacrifices it entailed. The road ahead would be treacherous, but they were prepared to face whatever challenges awaited them. Their first step was to rebuild their network of allies—individuals who had remained untainted by Maelstrom's influence.

"Let's see who we have." Sarah opened a list on her laptop. "We have contacts from various sectors. Everyone seems equally important."

"How many of them can be trusted though?" Alex asked.

"Three of these-" Sarah paused. "Eighty four."

"Wow, that's some ratio. But yeah, three is a good number. If we have to take Maelstrom down, each person will count.

They knew it was a delicate dance, as they sought to distinguish friend from foe in a world teeming with hidden agendas.

Sarah and Alexander knew that they were facing not only physical threats but also psychological warfare. Their enemies exploited their vulnerabilities, using fear, doubt, and manipulation to sow discord within their ranks. Trust became an elusive concept, as they grappled with the possibility that even their closest allies, like Luke, could be compromised. Amidst the chaos, Sarah and Alexander clung to each other, their love serving as a beacon of light in the darkest of times. As they realized all of these factors, they reaffirmed their commitment to one another and their cause, finding solace and strength in their unwavering bond.

With their ranks bolstered, Sarah and Alexander decided to orchestrate a series of covert operations to expose Maelstrom's activities.

"That's the only way. We have to penetrate the organization as much as we can," Sarah suggested.

"Let's send in Theo to where we think Maelstrom may be present in some form."

"Just Theo? Why not Luke?" Sarah asked.

"I don't know. I don't have a good feeling about him."

"You think he's dirty?"

"He could be. I know Theo isn't."

Sarah paused and then nodded.

"Let's start digging deeper into our network of informants. That's the best, and possibly the only way we can do something."

"Here's an encrypted phone. Call base and tell them." Sarah handed him a phone.

Alex called the HQ in Prague and briefed Theo about his next operation.

***

Months passed by as the battle waged on. Sarah and Alexander realized that defeating Maelstrom would require more than just exposing their crimes. They needed to strike at the heart of their power, dismantle their intricate network, and ensure that justice was served for all those who had suffered at their hands. With every victory, they drew closer to their ultimate goal. Maelstrom's grip on the world began to loosen as their operations were disrupted, their secrets laid bare for all to see. The public's support swayed in favor of justice, and the momentum shifted in Sarah and Alexander's favor.

But the cost of their fight weighed heavily on their souls. They had lost friends, witnessed unimaginable suffering, and endured personal sacrifices that would forever mark their lives. Yet, they knew that their struggle was not in vain. Every step they took, every blow they endured, brought them closer to a world free from Maelstrom's shadow. Sarah and Alexander had survived the depths of betrayal and emerged stronger. The final confrontation with Maelstrom loomed on the horizon, and they were ready to face whatever darkness awaited them together.

Chapter 11

The Endgame

Lublin, Poland

Sarah and Alex sat in a black Toyota Corolla. Sarah chugged on her drink as Alex held a military grade binoculars on his eyes. Sarah seemed calm. She chewed on her sandwich looking uninterested as Alex focused on what seemed like an abandoned building in the outskirts of Lublin.

A few seconds later, Alex lowered his binoculars and looked at Sarah who stopped chewing.

"How are you so relaxed? This could be it. This could put the final nail in Maelstrom's coffin," Alex exclaimed.

"We've been through so much, and we've tackled every situation so far. I'm sure we'll handle this one too," Sarah said casually.

"Wow. That's one way to look at it."

"I'm trying new things. Starting from this attitude." Sarah pointed to herself. She continued chewing. Alex smiled and gave her a peck on the cheek.

"I think it's time."

Sarah suddenly became vigilant. She sat upright and picked up her own pair of binoculars.

Ten men exited the building and took off.

"This is our chance. He must be in there with very few men," Sarah said.

"Let's go." Alex started the car and they went closer to the building. They stopped at a distance from where they could not be seen.

Sarah opened the glove box and took out her Glock. Alex took his from his holster. They exited the car and quietly moved toward the building.

"Theo, come in," Alex said on his radio.

"Theo here. Go ahead."

"Do you have eyes on the building?"

"I do."

"How many men are we dealing with?" Sarah asked.

"Thermal imaging shows six men. One in the bedroom, four scattered around the apartment, one outside."

"Copy," Alex said as they moved closer to the entrance.

"I'll keep you posted," Theo said.

Alex and Sarah entered the building from a broken gate at the back. They carefully walked through it and located the stairs.

"Do we have anyone guarding the stairs, Theo?"

"Negative."

Before Sarah could take step further on the staircase, Alex grabbed her arm and kissed her.

"I love you, Sarah."

Sarah smiled. She looked him in the eye.

"I love you too, Alexand-"

Sarah's words were interrupted by a gunshot that missed her head by inches. Alex quickly ducked and grabbed Sarah as the gunshots continued. The two hid behind a pillar as they heard two men shouting in Russian.

"Are you hit?" Alex whispered.

"No, are you?" Sarah panted.

"No, I'm good. They're coming. Get ready."

The two men went silent as their footsteps approached toward Sarah and Alex.

"What the fuck, Theo? Why didn't you tell us about them?" Alex whispered angrily on his radio.

"I didn't see them. They must be wearing those special suits. I still can't see them."

"Fuck. Sarah, listen. We need to take them out quickly and get to our primary target."

Sarah nodded.

"On the count of three, we leap toward that pillar take cover behind it, okay?" Sarah asked Alex. "One, two, three."

Alex and Sarah rolled over to the pillar beside them. It must have been three feet away but it allowed them to spot the two men. They immediately came out of their new hiding spot and shot at the men. Sarah aimed at the man standing closer to her and hit him right between the eyes. Before his partner could respond, Sarah shot him in leg too. Alex rushed over to the injured man and took away his gun.

"How many?" Alex shouted. The man did not respond. Alex repeated the question in Russian. The man smiled at him as Alex's

Glock pointed right at his nose. His smile revealed a missing front tooth.

"Go to hell!" The man growled in Russian. Alex looked at Sarah who gave her the nod. He shot in the forehead.

"Asshole." Alex spat on him.

"Let's go," Sarah said, her gun still in her hand.

They walked up the stairs carefully when suddenly, their radios went dead. Without giving it much thought, they proceeded to climb the dimly lit staircase. As they approached the third floor, they heard some muffled voices. Sarah, who was leading the way, turned to Alex and nodded. They topped for a moment and then continued. As they reached the third floor, they spotted an exceptionally large man guarding the front door. They backed off.

"Do you think he heard the shots?" Alex whispered to Sarah.

"No. Everyone had their suppressors on." Sarah lightly tapped at hers. "What's the plan?"

"We take him down silently. You have an amazing shot. Do you think you can take him down in the first attempt?" Alex asked.

"I think."

As they returned back, they saw that the man was gone. Before they could think any further, a large metal object hit Alex in the head. Sarah turned around to find the same man standing in front of her. He was twice the size of her. Sarah pointed the gun at him and fired but all she heard was a click. The man slammed her head against the wall.

****

Alex drowsily opened his eyes to find himself tied in chair next to Sarah. She was already awake and struggling to free herself as the gag in her mouth made her wheeze. The room was empty except for a table and an empty chair in front of them. They were facing a window that was painted black. The lights in the room illuminated it adequately. Alex tried to speak.

"Relax," a voice came from behind. A man walked up from behind them. He walked between the chairs and sat down on the one behind the table. It seemed like an interrogation. Alex and Sarah looked at him quietly as he settled himself in the chair. They immediately recognized who it was. "Mr. Davis, Ms. Morgan. You must know me." The man had a thick Russian accent. He had a light beard and short hair. His three-piece suit just added to his intimidating personality. It was Alexei Sirotkin. Alexei was Xavier's second-in-command. Alex and Sarah had been after him since they arrested Xavier. Even when Xavier was a free man, Alexei was the one who would run Maelstrom's operations and thus, it was imperative to bring him down to put a stop to Maelstrom's activities.

"Oh, forgive me." He stood up and ungagged Sarah.

"You piece of shit!" Sarah immediately shouted.

"Relax, Ms. Morgan." Alexei took out a cigarette. "I understand. You're just doing your job. But I am doing mine too. And in our line of work, one of us has to get killed." He lit his cigarette and took a deep puff.

"We're nothing like you, asshole!" Sarah yelled.

"Now, I know you came here to kill me, or maybe arrest me. But I wasn't going to go like Xavier. I would have rather killed myself than surrender to you. But now, since I clearly have the upper hand, I am neither getting arrested nor killed. In fact, you are the ones who will die today." He paused and took another puff before standing up and walking toward them. "Maelstrom cannot be stopped." He put his hand on Sarah's shoulder and walked out of the room. Before exiting, he told one of his men standing in the room to 'kill them once I exit the building and prepare to leave.'

Alex was now coming to his senses. He looked at Sarah who was tied in the other but her eyes were as determined as ever. She stared back at Alex and then dropped her head. She began crying. They could see their death right in front of their faces. Alex did not know what to say.

As Sarah and Alex prepared for their death, they heard heavy gunfire right outside the building. The man inside the room ran out the door to look at the situation. The gunfire continued for a few minutes before all went quiet. Sarah and Alex looked at each other. Before either one of them could speak, they heard someone enter the room behind them.

"You two just can't stay out of trouble, can you?"

"Theo?"

"Theo, indeed." Three other men followed Theo into the room. They were part of Alex and Sarah's team. All three along with Theo were heavily armed. Theo began untying the Alex and Sarah. "When the comms went dead, I knew something wasn't right, especially after the encounter you two had right at the beginning. We left the compound immediately and found your car a few meters away. Something told me I should go in. And so, here I am."

"What about Luke? Where is he?" Alex asked.

"Luke went back to Prague in the middle of the night. Didn't tell anyone. He's at the base as we speak," Luke said.

"And Alexei?" Sarah enquired.

"Dead. All of them. I'll show you the bodies on our way out," Theo chuckled once again.

The team rushed out of the building and reached their temporary base in the middle of Lublin before leaving for Prague the next morning. Sarah and Alex knew that Maelstrom was now done. There was nothing it could do now. With Xavier in jail, and Alexei dead, their operation was now decimated.

***

"And so, ladies and gentlemen, Maelstrom is no longer a threat to us. We'll be keeping an eye out for any resurfacing though. I want to thank you all. You risked your lives, your families, everything for the fight against this menace. I want to thank you. We couldn't have achieved this without you." Sarah addressed a room full people.

She went out of the room. Alex followed her.

***

Seven months later

Alex and Sarah sat by a lake in Northern Scotland. They grey sky and the slight chirping of birds made the surrounding vibrant and lively. Alex held Sarah's hand as they sat next to each other.

"I love you, Alex," Sarah said, not making eye contact.

Alex turned his head toward her girlfriend. She was the most beautiful woman he had ever seen and his love for her was just incomparable to anything he had ever felt before. Alex tightened his grip and smiled.

"I love you, Sarah."